MW00958243

Please enjoy this
gift book from

Kalamazoo Public Library
& Friends of KPL

Friends
Kalamazoo
Public Library

Dear Ballerina

written & illustrated by MONICA WELLINGTON

Holiday House • New York

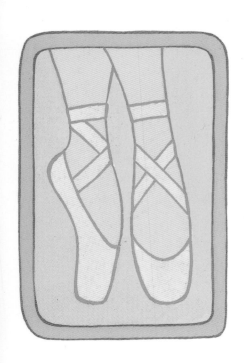

Copyright © 2019 by Monica Wellington

All Rights Reserved

HOLIDAY HOUSE is registered in the U.S. Patent and Trademark Office.

Printed and bound in July 2018 at Hong Kong Graphics Ltd., China.

The artwork for this book was created with gouache paints and colored pencil.

www.holidayhouse.com

First Edition

1 3 5 7 9 10 8 6 4 2

Library of Congress Cataloging-in-Publication Data

Names: Wellington, Monica, author, illustrator.

Title: Dear Ballerina / Monica Wellington.

Description: First edition. | New York : Holiday House, [2019] | Summary:
"A young dancer writes a letter to a ballerina she admires"— Provided by publisher.

Identifiers: LCCN 2018001410 | ISBN 9780823439324 (hardcover)

Subjects: | CYAC: Ballet dancing—Fiction. | Letters—Fiction.

Classification: LCC PZ7.W4576 De 2019 | DDC [E]—dc23 LC record available
at https://lccn.loc.gov/2018001410

1st position   2nd position   3rd position

For Lydia,
my little dancer
who has grown up
to be a beautiful,
strong ballerina

4th position

5th position

Dear Ballerina,
I dream of being
a ballerina like
you.

I love to dance.
I tiptoe in my
ballet slippers.

I bend and stretch to the music.

I love to jump and turn.
Dancing makes me happy.

I want to be
a beautiful, strong
ballerina like you, so
I practice every day.

I was excited to learn a part
for a real ballet onstage.
I worked hard in rehearsals.

I went to the costume
room for my fitting.

My tutu is
beautiful.

And best of all, you wore it too
when you were young like me.

I am dancing the same part
you once did.

I was a little nervous
when I was getting ready
for my first show.

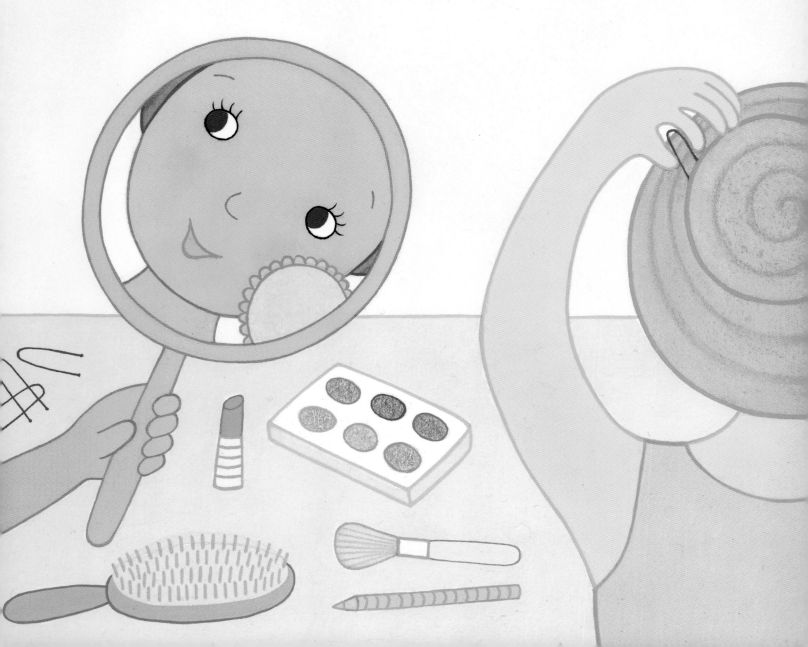

But while I waited for my
entrance, I watched you dance.

Dear Ballerina, you gave me inspiration.

Our tutus swirled together.

I love to dance.
One day I dream of
being an amazing
ballerina just like you.

Love, Little Dancer

Dear Little Dancer,
Follow your dream and
enjoy every moment!
Love, Ballerina

Epilogue

Nothing makes a ballerina feel more elegant than dancing in pointe shoes and a tutu!

Pointe Shoes

Pointe shoes are stiff, hard footwear covered in satin and made from layers of fabric, paper, and glue. Specialized shoemakers carefully fit them to a dancer's feet. Before wearing them, a dancer prepares her shoes to help break them in. She might pound them against a wall or bang them with a hammer so they won't be noisy on the stage. She might cut away part of the shank so the shoes conform better to the shape of her foot. She might rub the tip of the shoe in rosin so she won't slip and fall onstage. She protects her toes inside the shoe with paper towels, lamb's wool, or toe pads, and she sews on ribbons that she will tie around her ankles to help keep the shoes secure and snug.

A young dancer needs to work hard and become strong before she can dance on her toes in pointe shoes. For students, a pair of pointe shoes can last several months, but for professional dancers, busy with daily classes, rehearsals, and performances, a pair might last only one or two days before they become too soft.

When young dancers perform onstage with professional dancers, the children often write letters of appreciation to their grown-up colleagues. If a young dancer is lucky, she or he may receive a pair of signed pointe shoes in return!

Tutus

A tutu is a short, stiff, puffy skirt, often with an attached close-fitting bodice. The skirt is made of many layers of tulle fabric. The top layer usually has beautiful decorations, such as sequins, beads, rhinestones, and feathers.

Ballerinas wear tutus in many classical ballets, including *Swan Lake*, *Sleeping Beauty*, and *The Nutcracker*. Between performances, tutus are hung upside down to help them keep their shape.

The tutu was created at about the same time as the pointe shoe in the early 1800s. The first tutus were long, almost to the ankle. They have gradually gotten shorter and shorter to show the ballerina's legs and feet.

needle and thread

ballet slippers

leotard

scissors

pointe shoes

comb

notebook and pencil

Little Dancer's BALLET JOURNAL

makeup pouch

leg warmers

snack

bandage

scrunchie

mirror

practice tutu

hair elastics and pins

ballet bag

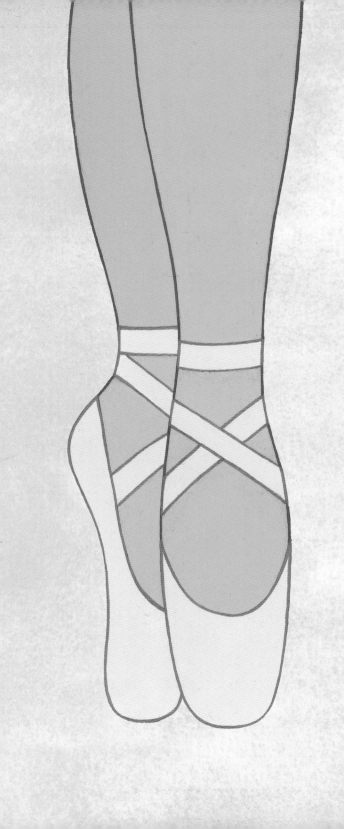